A CUP OF ZEN

21 Short Stories to Calm the Mind, Stop
Overthinking, and Find Inner Peace

The Zen Storyteller
Book 1

KAI TSUKIMI

To Kat

❀ Created with Vellum

A Free Gift For Readers 

A book can shift your perspective, but a ritual can transform your life. As a thank-you for reading, I'd like to offer you our exclusive *Zen Clarity Kit*; designed to help you clear your mind, refocus, and make Zen teachings a part of your daily routine.

What's Inside the Kit?

✔ **The Zen Morning Ritual Guide** – A simple daily practice to anchor your mind in stillness.

✔ **A 5-Minute Audio Meditation** – Gently guide yourself into a state of clarity and focus.

✔ **Zen Minimalism Wallpapers** – Subtle reminders to cultivate presence throughout your day.

 >> Scan the QR Code to download your free gift <<

Table of Contents

Introduction   xi

Part I
The Empty Cup

1   3
A Traveler's Weight

2   7
The Empty Cup

3   11
The Quiet Fisherman

4   15
The Master Who Insulted Him

5   19
A Master's First Day

6   23
The Desert Nomad

Part II
Beginner's Mind

7   29
The Teacher Who Forgot His Name

8   33
The Unfinished Circle

9   37
The Farmer Who Never Planted

10 41
The Cat That Walked Through Walls

11 45
Chop Wood, Carry Water—Again

Part III
The Habit of Habit

12 51
The Rider and The Horse

13 55
The Other Side of The River

14 59
The Temple with No Door

15 63
The Muddy Road

16 67
The Man Who Reached The Horizon

Part IV
Beyond the Self

17 73
The Painter and The Rain

18 77
The Bell That Never Rang

19 81
The Lantern and The Wind

20   85
The Jar of Ashes
21   89
The Weight of An Empty Bundle

Message From The Author   93
References   95

What Is Zen?

Imagine you're holding a cup of tea. It's full to the brim, so full that if you try to pour in more, it overflows. No matter how good the tea is, you can't take in any more.

Now, imagine that cup is your mind. Stuffed with opinions, worries, distractions, and things you think you "know." There's no space for new insights, no room for clarity. The more you cling to what you've already filled it with, the harder it is to experience anything fresh.

This is where Zen comes in.

Zen isn't about religion or memorizing deep philosophical concepts. It's about seeing things as they are—without overcomplicating them. It's about being here, fully present, without carrying the baggage of the past or the anxieties of the future.

Most of us are so caught up in our heads—planning, regretting, overthinking—that we forget how simple life actually is. Zen teaches us how to clear the noise and return to the moment. And what's one of the best ways to understand Zen? Stories.

What Are Zen Stories?

Think about the last time you heard a great story. Maybe it was a childhood fable, a parable, or even just a friend telling you about something wild that happened over the weekend. Stories stick with us.

Zen stories are like that. They aren't explanations—they're experiences. Instead of telling you *what to think*, they invite you to *see something differently*. Sometimes they're simple. Sometimes they're strange. Sometimes they make no sense at all—until, suddenly, they do.

A famous Zen master once said, "Pointing at the moon is not the moon." Meaning? Words, explanations, and theories can only point you in the right direction. But to truly get Zen, you have to experience it.

Zen stories are pointers—little glimpses into another way of seeing. They help you break free from rigid thinking, from the belief that everything needs an answer. Sometimes, the answer isn't an answer—it's just a different way of being.

This book is a collection of 21 Zen stories, each one designed to quiet your mind, simplify your thoughts, and bring a little more peace into your daily life.

How Do I Use This Book?

First rule: There are no rules.

Read this book however you want. Open it randomly, read one story a day, or finish it in one sitting. There's no single way to experience Zen.

But if you want a suggestion—try reading one story a day for 21 days. Let it sit with you.

Don't rush to "figure it out." Just let the story unfold in your mind. Some will make immediate sense. Others might confuse you. That's the point.

After each story, you'll find a simple reflection —a thought, a question, or a little practice to try in your own life. You don't need to force anything. Just let the ideas sink in.

Because the truth is, you don't have to "learn Zen"—you just have to remember what you already know deep down. And that starts with emptying your cup.

— *Kai*

PART I

The Empty Cup

EMPTY YOUR CUP SO THAT IT MAY BE FILLED.

Bruce Lee

1

A TRAVELER'S WEIGHT

A WEARY TRAVELER TRUDGED ALONG A
mountain path, his back bent beneath the

weight of an enormous bundle. Strapped to him were blankets, pots, books, and trinkets from places he barely remembered. His steps were slow, his breath heavy.

At the foot of the mountain, an old man sat beneath a cypress tree, watching the traveler's struggle.

"Where are you headed?" the old man asked.

"To the monastery at the peak," the traveler replied, shifting his load. "I seek wisdom."

The old man nodded. "A noble journey. But tell me, why carry all this?"

The traveler wiped his brow. "These are important things—things I may need."

The old man simply smiled and gestured to the path ahead. The traveler sighed and continued.

The path grew steeper, the air thinner. Each step drained him. Soon, his shoulders ached. His knees trembled. The straps cut into his skin. Finally, unable to bear it any longer, he dropped a pot by the side of the road. Then a book. Then a blanket.

By the time he reached the halfway point, he had shed nearly everything. His body, once burdened, now moved with ease. The wind felt crisper, the sky wider.

As he approached the peak, he found the old man already sitting there, waiting beneath another cypress tree.

The traveler gasped. "How did you—?"

The old man only smiled, then stood up and began walking toward a path that led further upward—one the traveler hadn't noticed before.

The traveler—exhausted from his journey—sat down to rest. As he was resting, he looked back down the mountain.

Far below, another figure struggled up the path, back bent beneath an enormous bundle.

Reflection

What are you carrying that no longer serves you?
If you dropped one story, expectation, or fear, how would your step change?

If you reached the peak, what would tell you that you had arrived?
Does the mountain confirm your journey, or do you?

———

A Moment of Zen

Hold a stone. Drop it. Feel the difference.

Think of a past event. Choose to let it go. Did it leave, or was it never there?

Go for a walk in silence. Notice what falls away and what remains.

2

THE EMPTY CUP

A traveling scholar arrived at a teahouse, seeking shelter from the storm. Rain lashed against the paper windows. Inside, all was still. An old tea master knelt behind the counter, setting out two cups.

The scholar lowered his dripping hood, shaking water from his sleeves. He placed a bundle of scrolls on the table, smoothing them with careful hands. His fingers tapped anxiously.

"I have read the sutras," he said. "Debated with monks. Memorized countless verses," he exhaled. "And yet, something is missing."

The tea master nodded, lifting the kettle. He poured into the scholar's cup.

The scholar leaned forward. "Tell me—what is the essence of Zen?"

The tea master poured until the scholar's cup was full. Then he kept pouring.

Tea spilled over the rim, streaming across the table, soaking the scholar's scrolls. He leapt up. "What are you doing?!"

The tea master set down the kettle. The only sound was the rain.

The scholar sat back down, gripping the edges of his robe. His scrolls were still soaking as the tea continued to trickle off the table and onto the floor.

He drank slowly. Eventually, the cup was empty.

Outside, the storm raged. Inside, a single drop fell.

Reflection

Where in your life are you still pouring?
Knowledge, worry, plans—some cups are
already full. What would happen if you
stopped?

Can you see the spill before it overflows?
What quiet overflow have you been ignoring?

———

A Moment of Zen

Pour water into a cup. Watch it until
it spills.

Hold your breath. Release it. Which
moment was full? Which was
empty?

Stand in the rain. Close your eyes.
When do separate drops become
whole?

3

———

THE QUIET FISHERMAN

A young boy stood at the shore,

watching an old fisherman cast his net into the dark sea.

"How do you know where the fish will be?"

The fisherman said nothing. He threw his net. It widened in the air, then fell, vanishing beneath the waves.

The boy frowned. "And if you catch nothing?"

The fisherman remained still, hands resting on the net, eyes on the black water. The tide whispered against the sand. The boy shifted his feet.

Minutes passed.

The boy exhaled. "What if there's a better way?"

The fisherman pulled in the net. This time, it was full. Silver flickered in the moonlight. He said nothing.

The boy opened his mouth to ask another question—but stopped. He watched as the old man cast the net again, into the shifting, unknowable sea.

The tide whispered. The net fell. The moon watched.

Reflection

Which is heavier—the weight of not knowing or the weight of needing to know?

If you cast your net into the unknown, what do you pull back?
Do you pull in truth, illusion, or only the movement of the water?

———

A Moment of Zen

Drop a pebble into water. Watch the ripples fade. What remains?

Write a question in sand. Wait for the wind. Read what is left.

Stand in the wind. Feel it touch you. Can you catch it?

4

THE MASTER WHO INSULTED HIM

THE GOVERNOR SAT IN THE courtyard, waiting.

He had heard much about the two great Zen masters—Renji and Kaito—who had traveled far to meet him. He was eager to learn. He wished to understand Zen.

When the masters arrived, the governor bowed respectfully. "I am honored to receive your wisdom."

Master Renji smiled. "You are an intelligent and perceptive man," he said. "I think you will make a fine student of Zen."

The governor nodded, pleased.

Then Master Kaito scoffed. "You've got to be joking."

The governor stiffened.

Kaito shook his head. "This man may hold power, but he wouldn't recognize Zen if it smacked him in the face."

The air went still. The governor's hands curled into fists, his pride prickling. No one spoke to *him* this way.

He took a slow breath, calming himself. Then, after a long pause, he smiled. "Thank you. I now know what to do."

The next day, the governor made a decision.

He did not build a temple for Renji. He built one for Kaito.

And he studied Zen under the man who had insulted him.

Reflection

Do you seek truth, or do you seek comfort?

**Who in your life challenges you to grow—
even when you don't like what they say?**

———

A Moment of Zen

**Think of someone who makes you
uncomfortable**—see what they
reveal.

When challenged, pause—are you
resisting growth?

Notice if you seek truth or comfort
and predictability.

5

———

A MASTER'S FIRST DAY

AT THE BREAK OF DAWN, A NEW MASTER
arrived at the monastery. He had studied for

decades, passed every test, and now—at last—he would take his place as head of the temple.

The monks gathered to receive him, lining the courtyard in quiet anticipation.

An old attendant bowed and said, "Master, your chamber is prepared. The students await your first teaching."

The master nodded. He stepped forward—but stopped. He turned, looking around the courtyard as if seeing it for the first time.

"Tell me," he said, "Where is the master's hall?"

The attendant hesitated. "You know the way, Master. You have lived here for many years."

The master furrowed his brow. "Have I?"

The monks exchanged glances. A young student stepped forward. "Master, perhaps you are joking."

The master looked at his hands as though they were unfamiliar. He took a breath, feeling the morning air on his skin. He touched the rough wood of the temple gate. The sun crept over the eaves, casting long shadows on the stone.

"Strange," he murmured. "It feels like my first day."

And without another word, he walked off—not toward the master's hall, but somewhere else entirely.

The monks stood in silence, watching him go.

The temple bell rang.

Reflection

If today were your first day, what would you see differently?
What disappears when you stop assuming you already know?

Which is truer—the path you remember or the path beneath your feet?
If knowledge fades but the wind still moves, which is real?

———

A Moment of Zen

Step outside at dawn. Breathe the first breath of the day.

Touch something familiar as if for the first time. Notice its texture, weight, warmth.

Walk a known path with new eyes. See what you have never seen.

6

——

THE DESERT NOMAD

A merchant crossed the desert, leading his camel toward a distant city.

For days, he followed the stars, charting his course by the sun. But when a great sandstorm came, the sky vanished, and his sense of direction with it.

When the storm passed, the desert had changed. The dunes had shifted. His tracks were gone.

A lone nomad sat nearby, warming his hands over a small fire.

"Excuse me," the merchant said, gripping his camel's reins. "Which way leads to the city?"

The nomad looked up. "Ah. A fine place. Have you been before?"

"No," the merchant said. "But I have heard of its wonders."

The nomad nodded. "Then how do you know it is ahead of you?"

The merchant frowned. "Because I was told the path leads there."

The nomad glanced around. "What path?"

The merchant turned. The sand stretched unbroken in every direction. No road. No city. Not even his own footprints remained.

His mouth went dry. "But... where do I go?"

The nomad smiled and poured tea into a clay cup.

The wind shifted. The dunes moved. The horizon did not.

Reflection

If every path vanishes, do you keep walking?
Are you lost, or have you simply arrived where you are?

What moves—the traveler or the horizon?
If the dunes shift and the wind turns, who or what is leading?

A Moment of Zen

Walk without direction. Let your feet decide.

Turn around in place. Watch the world move around you.

Stand in the wind. Feel it shift. Notice any movement.

PART II
Beginner's Mind

In the beginner's mind there are many possibilities, but in the expert's mind there are few.

Shunryu Suzuki

7

———

THE TEACHER WHO FORGOT HIS NAME

A YOUNG MONK WANDERED INTO A

bustling marketplace, searching for a renowned Zen teacher.

He came upon an old calligrapher, seated at a wooden stall, painting characters onto paper with slow, practiced strokes.

"Excuse me, elder," the monk said. "I seek the master who lives in this town. Do you know where I can find him?"

The calligrapher dipped his brush into ink. "A master? What is his name?"

The monk bowed. "I do not know. It is said he is a great teacher."

The old man pressed his brush to paper, forming a single elegant character. "Strange. I have lived here a long time, but I do not recall a master."

The monk frowned. "Are you certain?"

The old man lifted the paper and held it to the wind. The ink was still wet. The breeze smeared the character into nothing.

"I once had a name," the old man said, almost to himself. "But I seem to have forgotten it."

The monk stared at the empty paper.

The old man dipped his brush again.

The monk wanted to say something—but the next word never came.

The marketplace roared around them.

Reflection

If a name fades, what remains?
When ink vanishes and voices quiet, what is left
of who we are?

**Do you carry your name, or does it
carry you?**
If no one called you by it, would it still be
yours?

A Moment of Zen

Put hot water in a cup. Watch steam
rise. See it vanish.

Listen to a stranger say your name.
Notice how it feels.

Hold a blank page. Notice what is
there before ink touches it.

8

THE UNFINISHED CIRCLE

A WEALTHY NOBLE STOPPED AT A

roadside stall, watching as an artist painted cal-
ligraphy on silk.

"I hear you are skilled," the noble said. "Paint
me something worthy of my hall."

The artist nodded and took up his brush. With
a single stroke, he began to paint a perfect circle. His hand was steady, his ink dark and rich.

But just before he completed the shape, he
lifted his brush.

The noble frowned. "It is unfinished."

The artist set the silk aside. "Is it?"

The noble crossed his arms. "A circle must be
closed."

A cart rumbled past on the road, its wooden
wheel spinning, its edge blurred in motion.
The noble's gaze followed it.

He turned back to the painting. The ink had
dried. The gap remained.

His fingers twitched as if wanting to finish it
himself.

The artist took a fresh piece of silk, dipped his
brush—and began to draw another circle.

Again, he did not finish.

The wind stirred the silk. The noble said nothing.

Reflection

When does completion become excess?
A stroke too many, a word too much—when
does the masterpiece vanish?

What is missing, and is it truly absent?
A gap in the ink, a pause in the music—does
emptiness complete the whole?

———

A Moment of Zen

Draw a circle. Stop before it closes.
Notice the space.

Listen to a song. Focus on the silence
between notes.

Leave something unfinished today.
Let it be.

9

THE FARMER WHO NEVER PLANTED

A YOUNG GIRL WANDERED PAST AN OLD

farmer's field. The soil was rich, the sun warm, but no rice had been planted.

She stopped. "Grandfather, why is your field empty? It is time to sow."

The farmer nodded. "I thought so too. But I realized—I do not know what will happen."

The girl tilted her head. "If you do not plant, nothing will grow."

The farmer smiled. "And if I do?"

She scrunched her nose. "Then the rice will grow, and you will harvest."

The farmer looked at the sky. "Will there be rain?"

The girl hesitated. "I don't know."

The farmer gestured at the empty field. "Then how can I plant?"

The girl kicked at the dirt. She had no answer.

A breeze moved through the field, stirring the dry earth.

The farmer watched it pass.

Reflection

Does action bring certainty, or does certainty bring action?
If the future is unknown, do you plant the seed or wait for the rain?

Is waiting an act of patience or an act of fear?
When the field is empty, is it resting—or is it lost?

———

A Moment of Zen

Hold a seed in your hand. Feel its weight, its waiting.

Stand beneath the sky. Watch the clouds move, not knowing if they will bring rain.

Touch the earth. Sense what is already growing, seen or unseen.

10

THE CAT THAT WALKED THROUGH WALLS

A TEMPLE COOK CARRIED A HEAVY SACK
of rice through the courtyard, the weight

pressing into his back. At the garden's edge, he stopped before a high stone wall.

Sighing, he set the sack down. "Another ten steps to the gate," he muttered.

A black cat stretched beside him, tail flicking in the moonlight. It yawned, stood, and walked forward.

The cook watched as the cat passed through the wall.

He blinked in disbelief. The cat was gone.

Slowly, he picked up his sack and walked to the gate. The moment he stepped through, he saw the cat sitting on the other side, licking its paw.

The cat looked up. Its eyes caught the moonlight.

The cook turned back to the wall. It stood as solid as ever.

His fingers traced the rough stone.

A quiet chuckle escaped his lips.

The cat flicked its tail and walked away.

The cook did not follow.

The moon drifted behind the clouds.

43

Reflection

What is a wall, and what is a path?
If a barrier vanishes, was it ever truly there?

Do you follow the gate, or the cat?
Which path is real—the one you walk, or the
one you don't?

———

A Moment of Zen

Press your hand against a door.
Close your eyes. Feel its presence.

Watch a shadow move. Notice what
it passes through.

Walk around a familiar place. Find
an opening you've never noticed.

11

CHOP WOOD, CARRY WATER–AGAIN

A MAN LEFT HIS MOUNTAIN VILLAGE IN
search of enlightenment. He traveled far,

studied with wise teachers, meditated in silent temples, and sat for years in contemplation.

One day, he awoke with a deep and unshakable realization. At last, he understood.

He returned to his village, walking with the calm of one who has seen beyond the world.

An old friend greeted him at the gate. "You've returned," the friend said. "What have you learned?"

The man smiled. "Everything is clear now."

His friend nodded. "Good. We need more firewood."

The man picked up an axe and walked into the trees.

The wind rustled the leaves. The blade met the wood.

Somewhere, water flowed down the mountain.

Reflection

Does wisdom change the world, or only how you see it?
If the mountain remains, has the journey ended?

What is different, and what has only returned?
If the water still flows and the wood still burns, what has truly changed?

———

A Moment of Zen

Chop vegetables. Sweep the floor. Feel the rhythm of simple work.

Watch water flow. Notice where it comes from, where it goes.

Lift something. Set it down. Repeat.

Do not seek to follow in the footsteps of the wise; seek what they sought.

Matsuo Bashō

12

———

THE RIDER AND THE HORSE

THE DUST ROSE IN THICK CLOUDS AS
the horse galloped down the dirt path.

Its rider, a young man named Jiro, clung tightly to the reins, his heart pounding with the rhythm of hooves against the earth. The wind tore through his hair. His body swayed with every jolt.

Faster. Faster. Faster.

But something was wrong.

Jiro wasn't steering.

His hands gripped the reins, but he wasn't the one choosing the direction. The horse was moving on its own—charging forward as if possessed by something greater than itself.

He swallowed hard, glancing at the unfamiliar trees rushing past. Where was he going?

Ahead, an old farmer stood at the edge of the road, watching. As Jiro approached, the farmer cupped his hands around his mouth and shouted:

"Where are you going?"

Jiro barely had time to think before the words tumbled out:

"I don't know! Ask the horse!"

The farmer's laughter rang out behind him as Jiro disappeared down the path.

The road stretched on. The horse didn't slow. The landscape blurred.

Jiro gritted his teeth. He had been riding for so long—so fast—that he had never stopped to ask himself:

Had he ever been the one leading?

Slowly, he loosened his grip. He took a deep breath.

And for the first time, he pulled the reins—not out of panic, not out of habit, but with intention.

The horse hesitated.

Jiro pulled again.

This time, the horse slowed.

The dust settled. The trees no longer rushed past in a blur.

And as the world came into focus, Jiro realized: the horse had never been in control. He had just never tried to stop it.

Reflection

Where in your life are you moving forward without questioning where you're going?

What happens when you stop and take the reins?

A Moment of Zen

Notice when you're doing something just because "it's what you've always done."

Slow down an automatic habit—see what happens.

Take one mindful breath before your next decision.

13

THE OTHER SIDE OF THE RIVER

THE RIVER STRETCHED WIDE BEFORE him, its currents twisting and churning.

A young monk stood at the edge of the water, staring at the impossible distance.

How would he ever cross?

For hours, he paced the bank, searching for a way forward. No bridge, no boat, no stones to step across. No hope.

He sighed and slumped onto a hefty rock, burying his face in his hands.

Then, from across the river, a voice called out.

"Why do you look so troubled?"

The young monk looked up. On the far bank, an old teacher stood watching him.

Relief flooded his chest. If anyone could guide him, it was this man.

"Master!" he called. "How do I get to the other side?"

The teacher glanced up and down the river, then smiled.

"My son," he said, "you are on the other side."

The wind stirred the water. The current did not change.

The young monk stood still.

The river was no smaller than before. The distance had not lessened.

And yet, for the first time, he wondered if there had ever been a journey to make at all.

Reflection

What if the obstacles you see are only a matter of perspective?

What happens when you stop searching for "the other side" and look at where you are?

———

A Moment of Zen

Stop chasing and be still—see what changes.

Look at a problem from another angle—what else is true?

Catch yourself thinking, *"Once I get there..."* and ask, *"Where am I now?"*

14

THE TEMPLE WITH NO DOOR

A TRAVELING MONK HEARD OF A

beautiful temple hidden deep in the mountains, where the enlightened would gather.

After many days of climbing, he arrived at its stone walls. He circled the temple, searching for the entrance.

There was no door.

He frowned and walked around again. The walls were unbroken, covered in moss, stretching endlessly in every direction.

He waited. Perhaps someone would come out.

Days passed. The wind howled through the trees. The monk grew tired, cold, hungry. He pressed his hands against the stone.

"Why build a temple with no door?" he murmured.

A voice behind him said, "Who told you you were outside?"

The monk turned sharply. No one was there.

The wind moved through the trees. The walls stood silent.

Footsteps echoed from inside. They matched his own.

He stepped back, looking again—not at the temple, but at the space where he stood.

The moss was soft beneath his fingers. The air smelled of pine. Somewhere, a bell rang.

Reflection

Were you ever outside?
If the walls disappear, where do you stand?

What do you search for that has already found you?
If the path never ends, were you ever lost?

———

A Moment of Zen

Place your hand on a wall. Feel its texture. Step back. Notice the space around it.

Walk in a circle. Stop. Face a direction you did not intend.

Stand at a doorway. Step through. Turn around. Step through again. Repeat.

15

THE MUDDY ROAD

THE RAIN HAD NOT LET UP FOR HOURS.

Two monks walked along a muddy road, their robes damp and heavy with water.

As they rounded a bend, they saw a young woman standing at the edge of a deep puddle. Her silk kimono was spotless, but her path forward was blocked.

She turned to them and bowed. "Excuse me, would one of you be willing to carry me across?"

The younger monk stiffened. "Certainly not. Our vows forbid us from touching women."

Without a word, the older monk stepped forward, lifted the woman into his arms, and carried her across.

He set her down gently on the other side. She bowed deeply, thanked him, and continued on her way.

The two monks walked on in silence.

Minutes passed. Then an hour.

Finally, the younger monk burst out:

"I cannot believe you carried that woman. Have you no discipline? No respect for the rules?"

The older monk kept walking. "What did I do when we reached the other side?"

The younger monk frowned. "You put her down."

The older monk nodded. "Exactly. So why are you still carrying her?"

The rain had stopped. The path was clearing.

But only one of them had moved on.

Reflection

What burdens are you carrying long after they could have been put down?

What happens when you let go of something that no longer serves you?

———

A Moment of Zen

Notice when your mind lingers on something already finished.

In little ways every day, make the choice to let go.

When you feel resistance, ask: *Am I still carrying this?*

16

THE MAN WHO REACHED THE HORIZON

A MAN SPENT HIS LIFE CHASING THE
horizon.

Every morning, he rose with the sun and walked toward the place where the sky met the earth.

Years passed. His steps never slowed. Towns and rivers faded behind him. His beard grew long. His shadow stretched and shrank with the turning days.

One evening, as the sun dipped low, he looked up and saw it—the horizon, close enough to touch.

His breath caught. His journey was ending.

He took a final step.

The earth remained beneath his feet. The sky remained above.

The horizon had moved.

The man stood still.

For the first time in his life, he turned around.

Behind him, his footsteps stretched back forever, swallowed by the wind.

The desert was silent.

Somewhere in the distance, the horizon waited.

Reflection

Does the horizon move, or do you?
If the distance never ends, is it truly ahead
of you?

What disappears when you stop chasing?
If you stand still, does the path vanish—or does
something else appear?

———

A Moment of Zen

Walk toward a distant point. Stop.
Look again.

Turn around. Notice what was behind you all along.

Stand in an open space. Feel where
the sky meets the earth.

When I let go of what I am, I become what I might be.

Lao Tzu

17

THE PAINTER AND THE RAIN

A PAINTER SAT IN THE VILLAGE SQUARE,
carefully brushing ink onto a long scroll.

For hours, she worked—each stroke precise, each detail perfect. A river flowed through the mountains. A crane soared beneath the moon.

The villagers gathered in silence, watching.

The sky darkened.

A single raindrop landed on the scroll. Then another.

The painter lifted her brush. Black rivers bled across the page. The crane melted into the sky.

The villagers stepped back. The rain fell harder.

The painter did not move. She watched as the water carried her work away, drop by drop, until nothing remained but wet paper.

She set down her brush.

For a long time, she only watched.

Then, slowly, she reached out—and traced her finger along the trails the rain had left.

Her hand moved not against the storm, but with it.

The ink spread. The shapes shifted.

The villagers did not know whether she was painting, or only watching.

Neither did she.

Reflection

Is loss the end of creation, or part of it?
When the rain washes ink away, does the
painting disappear—or begin again?

What remains after something is undone?
If the image fades but the paper stays, was it
truly lost?

———

A Moment of Zen

Dip your fingers in water. Let it drip
onto paper. Watch the shapes form.

Wash your hands. Feel the water
touch you. Notice what it erases.

**Draw something on a piece of pa-
per.** Erase it. Repeat.

18

THE BELL THAT NEVER RANG

A NOVICE MONK ARRIVED AT A

secluded monastery, where an enormous bronze bell stood in the courtyard.

He asked an elder, "When does the bell ring?"

The elder smiled. "It does not."

The novice frowned. "Why have a bell that is never struck?"

The elder only swept the steps, saying nothing.

Days passed. The novice meditated, swept, carried water. But his eyes always returned to the bell.

One evening, unable to resist any longer, he approached it. He ran his fingers over the cold metal, tracing the carvings of swirling clouds.

His heart pounded.

He raised the mallet.

The night air was still. The weight of silence pressed against him.

He stood there for a long time.

In the end, he set the mallet down.

The bell remained silent.

The next morning, the elder found him sweeping the steps. He did not ask what had happened.

The wind passed through the courtyard, carrying the hush of something that had never been heard.

Reflection

Is an action meaningful because it happens, or because it doesn't?
If the bell had rung, would the silence still remain?

What is the weight of what you have not done? A word unspoken, a step not taken—do they echo, or do they fade?

———

A Moment of Zen

Lift an object you intend to use. Set it down without using it. Notice how it feels.

Stand before something you could change. Choose not to. See what happens.

Clap your hands—but stop just before they touch. Feel the space between sound and silence.

19

THE LANTERN AND THE WIND

A NIGHT WATCHMAN WALKED THE

quiet streets of the village, lighting lanterns as he went.

At each door, he paused to strike his flint, shielding the small flame with his hands. One by one, the lanterns flickered to life, casting pools of golden light against the dark.

As he bent to light another, he noticed a man sitting on the steps of a house, watching him.

"Careful," the watchman said. "The streets are dangerous in the dark."

The man smiled. "Are they?"

A breeze stirred. The lanterns shuddered.

In the shifting air, the watchman saw—for just a moment—the streets glowing pale beneath the moon, every house outlined in silver.

Then, in a single breath, the wind swept through the village and extinguished every flame.

The watchman stood still.

Darkness pooled around him.

But as his eyes adjusted, he saw the outlines of

rooftops, the soft glow of the sky. The village was not as dark as he had thought.

He turned back toward the house. The man was gone.

The night stretched on. The wind carried nothing but silence.

The watchman lowered his flint.

And walked on.

Reflection

Do you light the way, or does the way reveal itself?
If the flame vanishes but the path remains, was it ever dark?

What disappears when you stop trying to see?
If light shapes the world one way and shadow another, which one is true?

———

A Moment of Zen

Turn off the lights. Sit in the dark. Notice what remains visible.

Walk outside in nature at night. Look without a flashlight. Let your eyes adjust.

Stand beneath the moon. Watch how it lights the world without a flame.

20

THE JAR OF ASHES

A POTTER SHAPED CLAY AT HIS WHEEL,
hands steady as he worked.

A young apprentice watched, wide-eyed. "Master, how do you make something that will last forever?"

The potter smiled and placed the jar into the kiln. "Fire will decide that."

The apprentice waited eagerly as the flames roared, hardening the jar into its final form.

But when the kiln was opened, only a pile of ashes remained.

The apprentice gasped. "All that work—for nothing?"

The potter knelt beside the ashes and ran his fingers through them. "Nothing?"

He lifted a handful and let them drift through his fingers. The dust swirled in the air, catching the morning light.

The apprentice said nothing.

The potter stood and reached for more clay.

The wheel began to turn again.

Reflection

What remains when what you've made is gone?
If the jar turns to ash but the wheel keeps turning, where does creation end?

Is destruction the opposite of creation, or a part of it?
If fire reduces something to dust, has it undone the work—or completed it?

———

A Moment of Zen

Hold a handful of sand. Let it slip through your fingers. Watch where it goes.

Crumple a piece of paper. Smooth it out again. Feel what has changed.

Sit by a fire. Watch the smoke rise, drift, and disappear.

21

THE WEIGHT OF AN EMPTY BUNDLE

A MAN CLIMBED THE MOUNTAIN PATH at dawn, a bundle slung over his shoulder.

He had walked this road before. He had carried much heavier burdens.

Yet, with every step, his breath grew heavier. His legs ached.

At the bend in the path, he stopped. The rising sun bathed the trail in gold. He loosened the bundle and let it drop to the ground.

The knot unraveled.

Nothing was inside.

His chest tightened. He reached down and gathered the empty cloth, feeling its weight in his hands.

A voice drifted from behind him.

"Strange. You walk as if it were heavy."

He turned.

A traveler stood there, a heavy bundle across their back. His face was familiar, though he could not say why.

The wind stirred. The mountain stretched ahead. The bundle in his hands felt lighter than air.

He smiled. And kept walking.

Reflection

Do you carry what is heavy, or does carrying
make it heavy?
**If the bundle was empty, what made the
man's steps so difficult?**

When does letting go feel like holding on?
**If the burden is gone but your hands still
grasp it, is it truly gone?**

———

A Moment of Zen

Pick up an object. Hold it tightly. Set
it down. Notice what lingers.

Tie a knot in a piece of string. Untie
it. Feel the place where it once was.

Hold an empty bag. Put it on your
shoulders. Feel the weight and
lightness.

Message From The Author

Thank you for taking the time to read *A Cup of Zen*. My hope is that these stories have brought you moments of stillness, clarity, or even a small shift in perspective.

This book is part of a larger journey—to share the wisdom of Zen in a simple, accessible way so that more people can experience its teachings and find peace in their lives. In a world that often feels chaotic, even a single story can be a stepping stone to stillness.

If you found value in this book, I'd really appreciate it if you could write an honest review. Your feedback helps others discover these teachings.

<u>Scan the QR Code to share your thoughts.</u>

Thank you for being part of this journey.

— Kai

References

Kapleau, Philip. *The Three Pillars of Zen: Teaching, Practice, and Enlightenment.* New York: Anchor Books, 1989.

Mark Morse, trans. *The Gateless Gate: The Classic Book of Zen Koans.* Berkeley: Counterpoint, 2019.

Reps, Paul, and Nyogen Senzaki. *Zen Flesh, Zen Bones: A Collection of Zen and Pre-Zen Writings.* Boston: Tuttle Publishing, 1998.

Sekida, Katsuki. *Zen Training: Methods and Philosophy.* Boston: Shambhala Publications, 2005.

Shunryu, Suzuki. *Zen Mind, Beginner's Mind.* New York: Shambhala Publications, 2006.

Watts, Alan. *The Way of Zen.* New York: Vintage Books, 1957.

Yamada, Koun. *Zen: The Authentic Gate.* Somerville, MA: Wisdom Publications, 2015.